Tiger, Tiger

PAUL MASON

Illustrated by
Sean Longcroft

A & C BLACK
AN IMPRINT OF BLOOMSBURY
LONDON NEW DELHI NEW YORK SYDNEY

Contents

Chapter One	Shipwreck	7
Chapter Two	Heroes	12
Chapter Three	Holiday	17
Chapter Four	Uncle Amir	21
Chapter Five	Abandoned	27
Chapter Six	Searching	32
Chapter Seven	Hussein	37
Chapter Eight	Poachers	42
Chapter Nine	Flash Flood	47
Chapter Ten	Tiger Pit	52
Chapter Eleven	Ambush	57
Chapter Twelve	Trapped	62
Chapter Thirteen	Tiger Hunt	68
Chapter Fourteen	Home Again	73

Chapter One

Shipwreck

The rocks off the island had claimed another victim. Another ship was being pounded against the cold stone. Some townspeople gathered on the old wharf in the rain to watch. There was nothing they could do to help the ship – not in this gale. The coastguard had been called out. But in this weather, it could take ages.

Then the onlookers saw an explosion on deck. An eruption – a fireball blasting high into the sky. The townspeople yelped, and backed away.

'God help them,' one of them muttered.

But now, in the glow of the flames, they spotted something else. A flying shape, barrelling through the air towards the ship. Travelling like a rocket. Only this was no rocket.

'What on earth is that?' someone called out, pointing.

'Is that someone flying?' gasped one. 'Tell me I just didn't see that.'

Zephyr swooped down low over the ship, arms by his side. He cut through the storm, riding the currents of the wind like a hawk. He swerved to avoid the flames, and doubled back, checking out the situation.

'I've found the *North Star*, but I can't see anyone out on deck,' he shouted into his mike. 'Going in to take a closer look.' Zephyr abruptly halted his flight, and dropped to the deck. Even through his flight suit, the heat from the flames was strong. The ship shook under the pounding waves.

Zephyr grabbed the railing and looked over the edge. There was a gash down the side of the hull stretching below the water line. He could see a darkness spreading out through the water. Oil. And lots of it.

Things had just taken a turn for the worse.

Zephyr quickly passed on everything he'd seen to the others. He hoped they weren't far behind

He shot back into the air. He needed back-up, and he needed it fast.

'Aqua – you there?' Zephyr called into his mike.

'Coming up to the ship now.' Aqua's voice in his earpiece was a little jumbled. She was underwater, after all.

'Any chance you can control this swell – keep this ship from being crushed?'

'No problem,' Aqua shouted. Typical Aqua. Nothing was ever a problem.

Zephyr spotted Inferno racing over the shoreline, jumping from rock to rock, trying to get to the ship.

ZEPHYR NEEDED BACK-UP, **FAST**.

Inferno's legs hardly seemed to touch the surface. His body was on fire, flames trailing behind him in the wind. Zephyr still wasn't used to seeing his friend like this: the human fireball. As if he wasn't unpredictable enough.

'I need you up here, pal,' Zephyr shouted into his mike. 'This fire is getting out of control. I need you to switch it off.'

'On it!' Inferno shouted back, his microphone crackling. 'I guess I can save the day again.' Zephyr could picture Inferno's wide, cheeky grin.

Now Terra came online. 'I'm going to try and shift some sand under the hull, wedge it against the rocks a bit more. See if I can't get that ship more stable.' Zephyr could see her running along the shore. 'If I can force up a large dune, it might just block the hole and stop the leak.'

'Good idea,' Zephyr called back. No surprises there – Terra was always thinking.

Zephyr flew to the other side of the ship, and turned his body into the wind. He'd practised controlling the wind plenty of times. He could twirl the air like it was a top – but he'd never tried it in a gale.

Swallowing hard, he threw out his arms and pushed with everything he had. He hoped it was enough.

The captain on the bridge of the ship had already made the call to abandon ship. He'd made it ages ago – about the same time he had shouted 'Mayday!' on the emergency frequency. But that had been before the explosion. Before the fire. Half the crew were still trapped below decks with no way of making the lifeboats – if they were still alive at all. The walkie-talkies were out.

'Stay on the bridge!' he shouted at the first mate. 'I've got to get below, to the engine room.'

The captain swung open the door to the bridge, the wind knocking him back. He struggled out onto the gangway into the gale. Then, suddenly, it was calm. Completely calm. As if someone had pressed a button, and switched off the storm, just like that.

Chapter Two

Heroes

The friends were back at the abandoned airstrip, at the old Hercules plane that Mr Arturi had found for their base, everyone talking a mile a minute. Mr Arturi was finally able to stop pacing up and down and catch his breath. He'd been monitoring Factor Four's moves on the radio as they tackled the ship, helping them when he could. But the thought of his four students putting themselves in harm's way left him feeling a wreck – the way it had done last time, at the out-of-control forest fire.

'Well done, all of you,' he said, over and over. 'You were great.'

'Thanks, Mr Arturi,' said April drying her hair. 'Couldn't have done it without your help.'

'Yeah, it was fun,' Ian laughed. 'And that flame suit you rigged up for me was the business.' The others agreed. Their new suits had combined with their powers perfectly and had kept them safely disguised.

'The captain of that ship looked like he had seen a ghost,' Zaf chuckled. 'And when Ian and I spoke, he practically fell over.'

'What'd you say to him?' asked Tara.

'Told him that we were called Factor Four, and that we had it under control,' said Zaf, and grinned. 'I guess word is going spread pretty quickly.'

Zaf was right. Word did spread quickly. Newspapers up and down the country got hold of the story about the superheroes who had saved the ship and all its crew, and stopped an environmental disaster. The TV was swamped for days with eyewitness reports from the crew of the ship and the townspeople who had seen the whole thing from the dock. There were interviews with experts trying hard to work out just what powers these superheroes had. There was talk of a comic – maybe even a movie.

Factor Four had arrived.

'Check it out,' Ian said at their next meeting. To the groans of the others, he strutted about in a Factor Four T-shirt he had bought off the internet. 'I always knew I was going to be a star.'

***

At school, things took a while to quieten down. The idea that there might be real-life superheroes swooping around had created a bit of a buzz, to say the least. Gossip and chat flowed through the school hallways, but the four friends didn't bother to take part. Mr Arturi had suggested they all lie low. Ignore the emergency scanner and all the hype; put their heads down and concentrate on their work until the end of the term.

Zaf was following his advice. He was at a desk in the library, a pile of books by his side.

It felt good to be normal for a bit. Ever since he and his friends had breathed in the yellow gas from deep in the earth's core, things had been pretty helter-skelter.

Mr Arturi still wasn't close to working out just what the vapour had done to the four of them, or how exactly it had given them the powers of earth, wind, fire and water. But their science teacher had said he had a feeling they might develop even more powers. More power? Now there was a thought.

Zaf brushed it from his mind. He had a test to study for. Fractions – he liked fractions. At least you always knew where you stood with maths.

***

'How'd the test go?' Zaf's mum asked when he got home.

'Nothing I couldn't handle,' Zaf answered.

His mum closed her lap top and came over to give him a hug. 'I'm so proud of you – you know that, don't you? The way you work so hard. Both me and your ābbā.'

Zaf blushed. 'Yes, āmmā.'

'Well, guess who I just got an email from?' Zaf shook his head. 'Uncle Amir.'

Zaf's ears pricked up. Amir was his dad's younger brother – the tiger man. A park warden in a tiger reserve back in Bengal. Amir was one of his heroes. 'What did he have to say?'

Zaf's mum shrugged her shoulders. 'Oh, nothing much. He was only suggesting that we send you out to him to have a visit in these holidays coming up, and that you could bring some friends. I emailed back to say you probably wouldn't be interested in anything like that. Tigers are a bit boring – yes?' she said with a straight face.

'Are you serious?' Zaf's mouth hung open.

Zaf's mum laughed. She'd caught him, hook, line and sinker. Zaf had to chuckle. 'No, silly boy. I told him that your ābbā and I would discuss it.'

Now it was Zaf's turn to wrap his arms around his mum and give her a big hug. Uncle Amir. Bengal. Tiger Reserve. Now that sounded good.

Chapter Three

Holiday

'You're joking, right?' Tara was wide-eyed. 'A tiger sanctuary?'

Zaf grinned. 'Yep. My parents agreed I could go – if I raised half the money myself.'

Ian took a slurp of his juice. 'So, the four of us get to fly half-way across the world, hang out in the middle of a jungle and meet the fiercest big cat there is?'

'That's about the shape of it,' chuckled Zaf.

'Suits me,' Ian mumbled through a mouthful of sandwich.

'Would we get to help your uncle?' April asked. 'Do some conservation work?'

'For sure,' said Zaf. 'He said that was part of the deal. He needs some extra hands to gather data. It'll be like a working holiday.'

April pictured herself in the jungle, setting camera traps, measuring paw prints, helping tigers. It was too good to miss. 'I'm in,' she said. 'If I can convince my parents, that is.'

'I'm sure mine will say yes. But I'm not sure just how we can raise the money,' Tara sighed.

'That's simple,' said Ian spraying the table with crumbs. 'Car wash.'

'Have you any idea just how many cars we'd have to wash to get that kind of money?' April rolled her eyes. 'We'd need ten arms each!'

'Or to be superhuman,' said Zaf with a wink.

***

Even with the help of Mr Arturi, it took the four friends weeks of washing to get the money they needed. Row after row of cars. They got the permission of the shopping mall owners and their parents, and set up a gazebo in the mall car park with a sign that explained what they were doing. There were no shortage of customers.

Tara was the only one with a driver's licence, so she took the bookings and moved the cars. Under cover of the big tent Ian, Zaf and April got to work. Or rather, Ian, Zephyr and Aqua did.

'This doesn't seem right to me,' Ian grumbled. 'I'm the one doing all the hard work here while you two take it easy.'

Under April's hands, a tower of water rose up from the bucket at her feet and covered the car like a swirling blanket. 'Quit your whining and get scrubbing,' she laughed. 'Tara said we have five more to do before we finish today.'

Once Ian had covered the car in suds, April washed the soap off with a flow of water from her hand, and Zaf blasted the car dry with a mini tornado.

Ian shook his head. 'Couldn't I try to use a fireball – just once?' he moaned.

Chapter Four

Uncle Amir

After the long flight, the first thing the friends noticed when the door to the plane opened was the heat. It wrapped itself around them like cling film. Their clothes were soon clammy. Then came the line to get their passports stamped, and the struggle to drag their bags off the conveyor belt.

Finally the four were swept along in the crush and out through the airport doors.

Zaf spotted Uncle Amir waving at them in the crowd outside the arrivals hall. Good thing too – the place was a zoo. Crowds of relatives greeting family members, hawkers selling snacks, a chain of buses with conductors leaning out of open doors shouting destinations. There were brightly coloured motorcycle rickshaws, and an army of porters carrying luggage on their turbaned heads.

'Uncle!' Zaf called out. He weaved his way through the crowd. The others followed close by.

'Goodness, how you've grown,' Uncle Amir said, wrapping his arms round his nephew. 'Last time I saw you, I could throw you over my shoulder.' Zaf introduced the others and they shook hands.

Amir forced his way into the commotion and led them to a green jeep parked down the road. There was a tiger emblem on the side, and a man asleep in the driver's seat.

'Rajiv!' Amir shouted, and the driver woke with a start. Amir laughed. 'My good friend and assistant,' he said, introducing them. 'We had a long night, tiger-watching.'

'What did you see?' asked April.

Amir shook his head. 'Unfortunately, nothing. That's the problem. Things have changed lately.' He looked down for a moment, but then broke into a smile. 'But come, hop in the back. We've got a bit of a drive ahead of us to get to the park.'

Rajiv steered the jeep through the maze of traffic-clogged streets. Soon they were bouncing along a potholed country road, swerving to avoid cattle. They drove on through farm land and villages of huts with mud walls. Tara pointed out some workers bent double in the fields, up to their ankles in water, harvesting some kind of crop.

'Rice,' Amir explained when he saw the puzzled look on her face.

Finally, after what seemed like hours on the dusty road, they reached the edge of the jungle.

Tiger country.

The jeep passed through the gate to the national park and followed the road of dusty, red soil that cut through the forest. On either side of them was a web of trees, their trunks standing tall like statues, thick bush at their feet.

'If you're lucky you sometimes spot a tiger on this very road,' Amir said. 'Sometimes they even sit in the middle, and stop us passing.'

After that, the four friends kept their eyes on the road ahead, and on the tangle of green around them. But there was no sign at all of a great cat.

***

The tiger camp was a small bunch of camouflaged tents gathered around a clearing in the jungle, a few minutes' drive off the dusty road. Blink and you would miss

THERE WAS NO SIGN AT ALL OF A TIGER...

it. April and Tara shared one of the canvas tents, and the boys had another. The tents were large and pretty comfortable; each had little camp beds with mosquito nets, and a gas lantern for when the sun went down. Across the clearing was the dining tent and the shed that was Amir's office.

From the nearby village, Amir had arranged elephants for them to ride into the jungle on tiger safari. So, just after first light each day, they had a quick breakfast prepared by the cook in the dining tent, and then scrambled onto the great animals. Then the mahouts, the elephant drivers, gently guided the elephants into the dark forest, their strong legs crunching through the undergrowth.

Amir had to stay at camp each day – something to do with a project he and Rajiv were working on – but told them they were in the care of their best mahouts.

But things didn't work out as planned. The four friends didn't see a tiger on the first day. Or the day after that.

'Look at that!' Tara hissed loudly after they had set out again one morning. The elephants had reached the bank of a river. Just below them at the edge of the water lay a dark shape with a long row of teeth.

'Crocodile!' she called out to Zaf and April, snapping a photo.

'Gharial,' the mahout corrected her. 'Little bit different than crocodile. Very rare to see.'

'Also tiger prints,' said the other mahout pointing to the mud at their feet. 'Tiger was here for drinking.'

'Wow,' said Zaf. He took a picture of the pug marks with his camera.

But though the friends were enjoying the thrill of riding through the jungle on the back of elephants, they couldn't hide their disappointment from Amir when they got back to camp. The paw prints were the closest they had come to seeing a tiger.

Amir just shook his head when he heard their news. 'Perhaps tomorrow,' he said with a sigh. 'Now, please excuse me.' He went back to his office.

Zaf could see there was something troubling his uncle. But whatever it was, he was keeping it a secret.

Chapter Five

Abandoned

That evening after dinner, Amir wished them all a good night, and said he would see them in the morning. 'We have some field work to do,' he said walking over to his Jeep.

Rajiv was at the wheel, and Zaf saw there was a rifle by his side.

'Can we come?' asked April, following him. 'We'd love to help you collect data.' The others agreed.

Amir smiled. 'That's very kind. But this is something we have to do by ourselves. I promise to give you some work tomorrow when I get back.' Then he climbed into the jeep and drove away.

The four friends settled back in Zaf and Ian's tent to play cards instead. Around them they could hear the sound of the camp staff going about their jobs, closing down the camp for the night.

'Does it seem strange to you that we've been here almost a week, in a place where tigers are supposed to be protected, and we've not seen a single one?' Tara said, picking up a card.

'Ah, but maybe they've been there all along.' Ian widened his eyes. 'You can't see them, but they can see you.' He lifted his hands like claws and bared his teeth in a hiss. April shoved him off the bed. Ian lay on the floor, giggling.

'I'm afraid it's a sad statement on the world,' said April. 'Each year, tiger numbers are getting less and less. Pretty soon there might be none left at all.'

'Criminal poaching,' added Zaf. 'Crooks kill tigers for their skins, and their bones.'

'Bones?' asked Tara.

'For medicine,' said Zaf. 'Some seriously misguided people think you can make special medicine from tiger bones.'

'That's senseless,' muttered Ian.

'You said it,' April agreed. 'Senseless.'

***

28

The next morning, the sun was burning down and the air was already like a furnace before the friends got up.

'What happened to our wake-up call?' Ian yawned. Zaf realised he was right. Normally Amir shook them awake before it was light outside.

The two of them staggered out into the sunshine. Zaf noticed that Amir's jeep wasn't parked outside his office like it usually was. Either he had left early, or he hadn't come back last night.

Then Zaf noticed something else. The camp site was completely deserted. There was no sign of anybody in the office, the dining tent, or walking around the grounds. They were completely alone.

'Hello?' Zaf called out. Then again. Apart from the buzzing of the insects, and the call of birds from the trees, there wasn't a sound. No elephants, no mahouts, nothing. The campsite had been abandoned.

Ian emerged from the back of the dining tent. 'The kitchen's empty. No dirty dishes or anything. I don't think it's been used since last night.'

'I'm worried. It's not like my uncle to ditch us like this,' said Zaf. 'And where are all the others?'

Now Tara and April came out of their tent, rubbing the sleep from their eyes. 'What's up?' Tara mumbled. 'Did we sleep through the elephant trek?'

THEY WERE COMPLETELY ALONE.

Zaf shook his head. 'Looks like we all did. And there's something else. We're the only ones here.'

'What do you mean?' asked April.

'Look for yourself,' said Ian, gesturing to the campsite with a sweep of his hands.

The four friends finished getting dressed. Then, spreading out from the campsite, they wandered out down the road and into the jungle in all directions, going as far as they dared.

'Keep your eyes peeled,' said Zaf. 'You wouldn't want this to be the first time you come face to face with a tiger. Remember, their stripes are the perfect camouflage for the jungle.'

But it soon became clear that there was no one anywhere near. They plonked themselves down at one of the tables in the dining tent and wondered what to do now.

'I'm tired of waiting for something to happen,' said Ian at last. He got up and went to his tent. A few minutes later he came back with something bright red in his hands, and threw it on the table. It was his flame-proof suit.

'I thought I'd bring this – just in case,' he beamed.

The others looked at each other. 'I have to admit, I brought mine as well,' said Tara sheepishly.

'Me too,' said April.

'Well, I guess that makes four of us,' said Zaf. 'I think you're right, Ian, enough sitting around. Perhaps it's time for Factor Four to find out just what's going on.'

Chapter Six

Searching

On Amir's office wall they soon found a map of the tiger sanctuary showing the boundaries and tracks. Stuck to the map were little red pins with labels on them.

'Here's the campsite,' said Tara, tracing the map with her finger, 'and that must be the road we came in on.'

'The names on these pins must be the tigers, and where they were last sighted,' added April, reading one of the pins.

'So what's that circle mean?' asked Ian, pointing.

The others followed Ian's finger. Uncle Amir had circled a part of the park, close to the river – a fair distance from the campsite. Above the circle he had written 'Hussein!'

'Another tiger?' April suggested.

'I don't think so,' said Tara, 'or it would be labelled the same way as all the others.'

Zaf looked around his uncle's office. Everything was neat and tidy and in its place. On his uncle's desk he spotted a little box.

Zaf emptied the contents into his hand. There were two pins with labels. Two tigers. Taken off the map. Did that mean they were dead? Zaf shook the idea from his head.

'So what's our next move?'

'Find your uncle,' said Tara. She pointed at the circle on the map. 'And that looks like a good place to start. Your uncle must have circled it for a reason. Also it's near the river – perfect for Aqua to take a dip in.'

April nodded. 'Right! I could hit the river where it runs near the camp here, and ride downstream.'

'And I can follow things from above,' said Zaf.

'What about us?' said Ian.

'The last thing this forest needs is an out of control fireball cruising through it,' Tara laughed. 'You and I get to hold the fort for the moment, and see what we can find out by going through Amir's office.'

Ian groaned. 'But I brought my suit and everything.'

Zaf patted him on the back. 'I'm pretty sure you're going to get a chance to use it. Come on, April, let's get moving.'

Zephyr and Aqua jogged down the track that led from the campsite to the river's edge. Something told them that they needed to move quickly. Whatever had happened to Uncle Amir, it couldn't be good.

They reached the river, a ribbon of blue water carving its way through the jungle. At least it looked deep – plenty of room for Aqua to use.

'Watch out for gharial,' said Zephyr. Aqua thought he was teasing, and rolled her eyes at him. 'I mean it – keep safe. There's no Mr Arturi to guide us through this one.'

'Will do,' Aqua said, sliding down the muddy bank, and stepping into the water. Zephyr watched as Aqua's body changed in front of his eyes, turning from flesh to liquid. From his friend April into the raging current. All that was left was a silver wetsuit with the outline of a girl inside it.

'Testing, testing. Are you receiving? Over.' Zephyr tried his mike once Aqua had disappeared.

There was nothing. Then he heard a crackle in his earpiece. 'You can be such a Poindexter sometimes,' Aqua laughed, her voice blurred by the water. 'Heading downstream now.'

Zephyr leapt into the air and blasted upwards, his arms by his side, his ears popping, his mask pressed hard against his face.

'I'll go on ahead and radio when I see something,' he said.

When he thought he was high enough, Zephyr levelled out and followed the stretch of water below. He reckoned he was just below 7,000 feet. About the height a small plane might go.

If there was something where Uncle Amir had circled it, all he needed to do was keep the river in sight. Spread out before him, the jungle was like a carpet of rich green.

Zephyr looped the loop, and again, shooting up high into the air, and back-flipping around. He couldn't help himself. Ever since the awakening of his powers he'd been working on his skills. Now, he barrel-rolled – spinning through the air like a dart about to hit its target. He spotted some parrots on the wing far below him, and gave chase. The startled parrots squawked and changed tack.

Then, out of the corner of his eye, he spotted it. What looked like another campsite. A cluster of tents in a clearing next to the river. Zephyr allowed himself to drop down, bringing the camp into view. There were three jeeps parked nearby.

And if he wasn't mistaken, one of them was Uncle Amir's.

Chapter Seven

Hussein

Back at their camp, Ian and Tara were still in Amir's office, rooting around for information on Hussein. Not that they'd found any. What they did discover was a chart showing the number of tigers in the sanctuary. And year, by year the numbers were getting smaller.

'At that rate, there'll be none left in a few years,' Ian muttered.

'Some of those deaths would be natural,' said Tara. 'But look at that column.'

Ian followed where Tara was pointing. Under 'fatalities', there was a column headed 'poaching' and each year that number was getting bigger.

Just then, there was a clatter from the kitchen next door. Ian and Tara froze. Doing his best to keep control,

Ian burst through the door and raced into the kitchen, hands raised, ready to unleash a fireball. But when he saw who it was he smiled. It was the camp cook, a sack of rice in his arms. The cook looked more startled than he was.

'What's going on?' Ian gestured to the camp. 'Where is everyone? Where did you go?'

The cook raised his finger to his lips – telling Ian to be quiet. He looked around with fear in his eyes.

'What is it?' Tara whispered. 'What are you afraid of?'

The cook shook his head, and hissed something at them in his own language. He didn't speak any English. Ian and Tara understood one word though. 'Hussein.' Then the cook raised his arms like he was firing a rifle. He pulled the imaginary trigger, first at Ian, then at Tara, and then at himself. The cook repeated the word 'Hussein.'

Ian and Tara didn't need to be expert in languages to work that one out.

The cook made apologetic noises that suggested he was sorry he couldn't help them, and left as quickly as he had come, taking the food he had come for.

Tara ran back to the office and grabbed her headset. 'Guys!' she blurted into the mike. 'There's something you need to know…'

At the campsite by the river, Hussein leaned back in his chair and watched his men at work as they stretched a tiger skin between two trees. The skin with its proud, black stripes that just the day before had been part of a living, breathing tiger.

Hussein stroked his beard while he watched. This trip was working out well. They had caught two tigers already, using a single tiger pit. He and his men would catch one more. Then they would let the skins dry for a few days and pack up camp. Go to the city and sell the skin and bones on to a dealer for a big pile of cash. The dealer would clean them some more, and arrange to have them smuggled over the border.

One day he would move up the ladder, thought Hussein to himself. Become a dealer. That was where the big money was. Then he wouldn't have to get his hands dirty. He was tired of being just a foot soldier.

'Be careful there!' he barked suddenly. 'I don't want that skin damaged.' Hussein's hand touched the revolver at his side. He couldn't help it. It was instinct. He lived by the gun – as the people in this park were quickly finding out. His men swallowed, and kept their eyes on the ground. It was best not to argue.

From behind Hussein came a growl. A voice full of fury.

'Don't want that skin damaged – listen to him, Rajiv.' Amir and Rajiv were roped to a tree. They'd been there for hours. Amir spat on the dusty ground. He tried to shift his arms so that the rope didn't cut into his skin.

'As if that murderer could possibly harm that tiger any more.'

Rajiv didn't share his friend's bravery, and said nothing.

Hussein got up from where he was sitting and marched over to Amir. 'Just for that, you can go without water for the rest of the day. Remember, I still haven't decided whether I'm going to let you live yet, park warden,' he hissed.

If Amir was worried, he didn't show it. 'Coward,' he spat.

Hussein leant down and grabbed Amir round the jaw, forcing his face up. 'You should have run when you had the chance. All your friends did.' Hussein chuckled, a hacking laugh that showed off a mouth full of gaps. 'They won't be coming to help you. No one will.'

Chapter Eight

Poachers

Zephyr banked right, and slowed down, dropping steadily to tree level. He darted through the thick web of branches, and touched down close to the river bank, just downstream from where he'd seen the campsite. After what Tara had told them about Hussein, they needed to be alert. Super powers or not, none of them were bulletproof.

Zephyr clambered to the side of some boulders on the river's edge. 'Aqua, you there?' he whispered into his mike.

'Still going with the flow,' came the reply. 'This river's running fast. Shouldn't be long.'

'Look for me on the bank to your left,' said Zephyr. He waited for a little while, keeping his eyes on the

water. Not that you had any chance of spotting Aqua when she'd gone liquid. He remembered how she'd told them about the first time she'd transformed. She had been swimming in the sea when a shark had come looking for a snack – only it never found her. Only sea water.

Just then, a part of the river started to swirl. A head emerged, then a silver wetsuit, and arms that looked like they were made of water.

Aqua stepped out onto the river bank, and transformed into flesh again. She climbed up the bank and crouched down beside Zephyr.

'Glad you could make it,' he whispered.

'Had to deal with some hairy rapids.' Aqua wrung out her wet hair. 'What's the plan?'

'The camp is just around that bend there, right next to the river,' said Zephyr, pointing. 'You flow downstream and see what you can find out from the water. Get a good scope on how many men we're dealing with. What kind of equipment they've got. Try and find out where Amir and Rajiv are. I'm going to fly in low – under the cover of the trees.'

'Remember what Tara said,' Aqua reminded him. 'They're probably all armed.'

'We'll be in and out,' promised Zephyr. 'No fancy stuff. We'll come back later when it gets dark. Besides, we've got to let Inferno crash this party or he'll never speak to us again.'

Aqua slipped into the water and was gone. With the current as strong as it was, she'd make the camp in no time.

Zephyr sprung into the air, and darted back into the forest. As he flew through the canopy of trees, flocks of startled birds burst from their branches, chattering and screeching. Zephyr hoped they wouldn't give the game away.

As soon as he could see the tents in the clearing, Zephyr threw on the brakes, and grabbed hold of a large branch, swinging himself behind the thick leaves. He could see the camp, but the men wouldn't think of looking up this high. At least, he hoped they wouldn't.

From his perch Zephyr had a good view of the campsite. He could see a couple of poachers busy around the camp, loading things into the jeeps. There might be more men in the tents or down by the river – he couldn't be sure.

Zephyr's heart started thumping. There, lashed to a tree trunk on the edge of the camp, were Uncle Amir and Rajiv. Prisoners.

Amir looked like he had been roughed up. His face was bruised and his head hung down. Rajiv didn't look much better. They looked like they'd been there all night.

Then from the river bank came another man. Dark glasses, dark beard, drying himself with a towel. He was calling out orders to the others. Hussein, it had to be.

Zephyr couldn't hear what Hussein was saying, as he was too far away, so he clambered up to a closer branch, on the edge of the clearing. Then it happened.

There was a loud crack, and suddenly Zephyr was falling. For a moment he forgot he could fly, and a moment was all it took. He bounced off the branch below, then another, crashing through the leaves, snapping twigs, arms clawing uselessly. He hit the ground with a loud thud, and rolled around on the forest floor, winded and gasping for breath.

The men in the camp froze and stared at the strange intruder. A figure in a blue body suit, twisting in the dirt. Amir lifted his head.

Hussein was the first to react. He reached for his holster and whipped out his gun. 'Get him!' he ordered.

Chapter Nine

Flash Flood

Zephyr's head hurt. Everything had gone blurry. Slowly his breath came back to him, and he pushed himself gingerly up off the ground. He adjusted his goggles just in time to see two men run towards him across the clearing, with Hussein close behind them.

Zephyr wobbled to his feet, and turned back to the forest, but he was too unsteady to fly, and too sore to run. The men were bearing down fast. There was a loud crack, and a whine. Then another. Little puffs of dirt kicked up near Zephyr's feet. They were shooting at him! He had to get out of here.

But then came a roar from the direction of the river, and from nowhere, a torrent rushed over the clearing, crushing tents, slamming jeeps, and swatting the men

to the ground like they were scarecrows. Hussein's legs were whipped from under him. Amir and Rajiv were drenched.

Hussein and his men leapt to their feet, as the flood water retreated, but the intruder was gone.

Hussein fired uselessly into the forest, and screamed at the sky. He was sure the strange man had been spying on them. He hadn't been a villager, that was for sure. But what on earth had happened to the river? A couple of his men were standing at the river bank staring at the water – they had never known anything like it.

Hussein quickly went and checked on the tiger skins in the trees – at least they were still dry. Their payday was safe.

'Change of plan. Get this place packed up!' Hussein snapped at his men. 'After we catch that tiger tonight, we move out!' He spat on the ground. 'And then we get rid of these two.' He gestured at his prisoners.

Zephyr blasted his way through the forest and up into the sky, faster than he'd ever flown before. Then again, he'd never been shot at before. He slowed down when he was well out of range.

'You OK?' a voice fizzed in his ear. It was Aqua.

'Just about. Thanks for saving my skin.'

'No worries.'

'Heading back to camp now.' Zephyr exhaled loudly. That had been far too close for his liking.

***

Back at their campsite, Zaf and April told the others about everything that they'd seen downriver. The encounter with Hussein had left them feeling shaky – not that they were going to give up.

Ian and Tara were trying to piece everything together. Ian paced up and down the dining tent. 'So, this Hussein heads a tiger-poaching outfit. A real nasty piece of work. A few days before we turn up, he brings his gang to the park and begins operations.'

'Amir and Rajiv track him down,' Tara continued, 'only they get caught. Hussein threatens all the others and gets them to clear out, or else.'

'And who can blame them. If I was a poor villager worried for my family, I wouldn't want to cross him either,' Zaf sighed.

'Remember, I overheard Hussein tell his men they're going to bait their tiger pit again tonight. There's going to be another dead tiger. And that's not the only thing.' April swallowed. 'I think he has the same plan for Amir and Rajiv.'

'Not if Factor Four have anything to say about it, he doesn't,' Ian snapped.

Zaf nodded. 'Too right.'

'We go back. And we send Hussein packing,' April agreed. 'But we'd better act quickly. You two had better get changed,' she said to Ian and Tara.

Trying their best to think about what Mr Arturi would do in this situation, the four friends tried to think up a plan. One that rescued Amir and Rajiv, saved the tiger, and put Hussein and his crew behind bars. Secretly each of them wished their science teacher was with them now. But that wasn't going to happen.

They decided Zephyr and Aqua would get back to Hussein's camp through the air and downstream the same way they'd done before.

'And look what I found,' said Ian, pushing a motorbike, 'hiding in one of the sheds. Tara, we can use this.'

The motorbike looked old and dusty. Tara kicked the wheels. They were still hard. 'Do you even know how to ride this thing?' she asked.

'Er, no,' Ian admitted.

'Then it looks like I'll be doing the driving. My cousin showed me how on her farm.' Tara swung her leg over the saddle and turned the ignition key. Then she jammed down on the starter pedal. The motorbike spluttered and died. Tara lifted herself off the seat and jumped down on the kick starter again. With a cloud of smoke, the bike rattled into life.

'OK,' said Zaf. 'Good luck – and keep yourself safe. Don't want any of you falling out of trees,' he added with a grin.

Chapter Ten

Tiger Pit

The tiger pit was deep, with sides that rose up sharply. It had taken Hussein's men the best part of a day to dig it. But it had been worth it.

In the old days, the bottom of the tiger pit would have been lined with sharp stakes. But stakes ruined a good tiger skin, and Hussein didn't want that. Instead, once the tiger fell in to this pit and couldn't get out, they would shoot it with a dart. Put it to sleep, forever.

In the last of the daylight, Hussein's men finished covering the mouth of the pit with branches and leaves. Then they swept the ground to cover up any tracks. Even if you looked really closely, you would have no idea of the danger that lay below.

Finally, the men hung a slab of meat on a rope suspended just above the pit. The tiger would follow its nose down the track, smell the blood, and move in for an easy meal. You didn't need to be a rocket scientist to work out the rest. The pit would be a tiger grave.

'Good,' Hussein growled as he watched his men finish. 'Now, we wait.'

Hussein ordered his crew to pull way back, well out of range. They didn't want their scent to scare the big cat away.

Hussein tested his night-vision goggles. 'Hold your positions,' he muttered into his radio. 'And make sure those prisoners are secure.'

'Yes, boss,' came the reply from the man standing guard at Hussein's camp. Dutifully, he went over to Amir and Rajiv and checked on the ropes. There was no way those two were going anywhere.

The man felt sorry for them. But they should have tucked their tails between their legs and ran when they'd had the chance. Hussein didn't ask twice.

'Water,' Rajiv gasped. 'Please.'

The man thought for a moment. Hussein's orders were 'no water'. But what harm could one cup do? It would probably be the last thing to pass their lips.

'OK,' the man muttered, grabbing his water can and heading for the river. 'Just wait.'

The man laid down his rifle on the river bank, and knelt down with his water can, dropping it into the river by its straps. In the gloom, it looked like the river was running like normal – no more freak waves.

The man stood up to go, but the straps on his bottle went tight. The bottle must have caught on something. He tugged at it again. Definitely stuck. He bent over and gave it a hard yank with both hands.

Suddenly it was as if the river had come alive. A shape burst from the water like a ghost, standing tall. It grasped at him. The man could feel hands tightening around his forearms, but there were no hands, just river water.

The man screamed in terror as, without warning, he was dragged forward and thrown into the raging water of the river.

He clawed his arms at the surface as he was swept downstream and away from the camp. He shouted out into the dark as he rushed along.

Aqua clambered from the water. 'All clear, the guard's gone for a swim.'

'Roger that,' replied Zephyr. He swooped out of the darkness like a hawk, and hit the ground running.

Amir and Rajiv raised their heads at the sound. Were they delirious or was some blue figure now standing in front of them, with a mask over his face? They felt their

IT WAS AS IF THE RIVER HAD **COME ALIVE**!

ropes being loosened, and then a surge of pain, as blood rushed back into their limbs.

'Are you both OK?' Zephyr asked.

'Water, please,' gasped Amir.

A second masked figure came towards them in the gloom. 'Here you go.' A girl's voice. The figure knelt down and handed them a water bottle. The two men drank greedily.

'Who are you?' Amir found his voice.

'There's no time,' said Zephyr. 'You need to get into your jeep and reach the authorities. Are you strong enough to drive?'

Amir nodded. 'But what about Hussein and the others?'

'Don't you worry about that,' Zephyr spat. 'We'll take care of them.'

Chapter Eleven

Ambush

Hussein switched on his night vision goggles and scoured the forest. In the shadows of green and black he could see his men dotted around the trees, their eyes glowing. But no tiger, just the buzz of insects.

The big cat would come, he was sure of it. Then they would have three pelts for sale. More money than villagers in these parts would see in half a lifetime.

Hussein had heard that further up the poaching chain, the big businessmen at the top were stockpiling tiger skins and bones. Waiting for the animals to go extinct, when the price would skyrocket. Hussein thought he was ruthless, but that was colder than cold.

Then, over the sound of the forest Hussein thought he could hear something else coming from the direction of the road - the sound of a jeep leaving the camp. What was that foolish guard doing? He'd scare any tigers away.

Hussein hissed into the radio. There was no response. He tried again. 'Go back to the camp and find out what's going on,' he grumbled to the man crouched next to him. 'Radio as soon as you get there.' The man nodded and crept off into the darkness.

Hussein waited for the man to get back to the camp. Waited for word to come. Again, there was just the noise of the jungle. He tried to reach his man by radio, but there was no answer.

First the spy that afternoon, and now this. Something was wrong. What if that foolish game warden and his assistant had somehow got loose?

Hussein ordered his men to stand by with their rifles drawn. 'Stay alert. Keep your eyes on the pit.'

He pulled out his revolver and released the safety catch. Keeping low, he crept through the trees, back towards the camp.

He hadn't got far when the ground below his feet began to shake. At first Hussein thought he'd stepped on something – an animal. A snake? With horror he moved quickly, back the way he came. But it wasn't an animal. The trees around him were shaking too.

It was an earthquake.

The ground rumbled and rolled. It juddered from side to side. Hussein grabbed hold of a tree for support. In the darkness, his men called out to each other. Through his night vision, Hussein could see the terrified looks on their faces as they tried to cling onto something that wasn't moving.

Birds squawked in the branches above, and took to the sky. A small herd of deer burst through the bushes and vanished.

Then it stopped. For a moment the jungle was quiet, except for the frightened jabbering of Hussein's men. They were spooked.

'Back to your places!' Hussein ordered.

'First the river goes angry, and now the ground,' one of them muttered. 'I don't like this.'

'You'll like it less with my boot on your backside!' Hussein growled. 'It was only a small earthquake, you fool! Go and check on the bait, then see what's happening back at camp.'

The man shook his head, but did as he was told. He edged his way towards the pit, as close as he dared. With the branches covering the pit, it was hard to see where the opening was.

The man could see the hunk of meat swinging gently from its rope. It was still in place.

'All OK, boss,' the man called back.

"FIRST THE **RIVER** GOES ANGRY - NOW THE **GROUND**!"

Then it hit. Another sudden jolt from the ground, forcing the man back on his heels. A hard jerk. Again, he was pushed backwards. 'Boss!' he cried out. The ground rumbled as if someone had taken hold of it and was shaking it like a rug. The man stumbled - one step too many. There was a crack of branches, a snapping of twigs, then a terrified scream as the man plunged into the pit.

The earthquake stopped.

'Get that idiot out,' Hussein screamed at his men. 'Quickly!' What chance was there of catching a tiger now?

Chapter Twelve

Trapped

From her position near the clearing, Terra waited until all of Hussein's men were gathered around the edge of the pit, reaching down to rescue the man inside. She planted her feet firmly on the ground, and felt the power of the earth flow into her body. She lifted her arms above her head, and brought them down.

The ground buckled under her command. Terra swept her arms to the side, making the earth roll.

The men stood no chance. Their legs crumpled beneath them. They collapsed into the pit, arms flailing, and were gone.

From the bottom of the pit came groans.

'Now I guess you know what it feels like,' Terra whispered.

While his men were trapped, Hussein ran through the trees, away from the pit. Something very bad was happening in this place. He needed to get out. Hussein pushed branches aside, clawing at the green, using his night vision to find a path through the undergrowth. He'd get to the camp, grab the two pelts that were drying and all the equipment he could, and beat a retreat to the city. The others would have to fend for themselves.

A voice came out of the darkness. 'Going somewhere?'

There in front of him was a figure. Unless the night vision was fooling him, the figure was wearing a mask. Like the spy they'd seen that afternoon. Hussein whipped out his gun, and there was a sudden flash. Flames burst over the figure, right in front of his eyes. Hussein was blinded. With his free hand, he pushed his goggles off his face, and fired where he'd seen the figure. But the masked man was gone. The flames had disappeared.

Hussein spun around, his eyes struggling to cope with the dark. He fired wildly again.

'Naughty, naughty,' Inferno laughed from his hiding place. 'You want to stop doing that.' He raised his arms and shot a jet of flame at Hussein's hand – the one holding his gun. Hussein yelped and dropped the weapon to the ground.

'Too hot to handle, eh?' Inferno sneered. 'How about this?'

A stream of flame blasted into the night, just above Hussein's head. Then another that scorched his shoes. Hussein bolted through the jungle, back the way he'd come.

Back towards the pit.

Hussein ran blindly, his heart thrashing, his lungs struggling. A blast of flame scorched past his head, forcing him to change direction.

Out of the corner of his eye he saw the figure of fire on the path behind him. He could hear the crackling of the flame. It must be a ghoul come to feast on his flesh. Punishment for all the tigers whose lives he'd taken. What else could it be?

Heat beat against his back, driving him on. Hussein's legs screamed in pain as he stumbled through the bushes. Branches clawed at his face.

Hussein reached the clearing. From the terrified shouts of his men inside, he knew the pit was right there in front of him. He fell to the ground in a tumble to stop himself from dropping, and rolled, over and over, stopping at the mouth of the hole, fingers grabbing at the dirt.

Hussein pushed himself to his knees and spun around, searching the darkness. There was nothing.

'Looking for me?' Inferno hissed in the dark. He burst into flame at the edge of the clearing. Hussein could see him clearly now. Arms, legs, hands. It was as if they were all made of fire.

Hussein whimpered and dropped his head. There was no escape. 'Who are you?' he moaned.

'A friend of tigers,' Inferno spat. He raised his arm, and a blast of fire hit the ground in front of Hussein,

IT MUST BE A *GHOUL*, COME TO FEAST ON HIS FLESH!

sending him flying back, down into the pit, right on top of his men.

Inferno strolled up to the edge of the pit. He looked casual but he wasn't taking any chances; one of the men might still be carrying a rifle. He walked round the pit, ignoring the groans of the men inside, blasting a trail of flame onto the ground around it as he circled.

'NOT BAD, INFERNO. NOT BAD.'

With a click of his fingers, Inferno switched off his own flames, leaving the pit surrounded by fire. He checked the clearing, making sure the rest of the forest wasn't going to catch alight.

Tara emerged from the dark, and gave him a hug. Her skin had transformed back from earth into flesh. 'Not bad, Inferno,' she smiled.

'Not bad yourself,' said Ian. In the distance they could hear the roar of engines, coming closer.

Chapter Thirteen

Tiger Hunt

Flying above the forest it was easy for Zephyr to spot the tiger pit. A circle of fire blazed in the clearing like a beacon. Zephyr could also see a procession of headlights coming down the jungle road – Uncle Amir and the police.

Zephyr dropped down and swooped into the clearing. 'Hussein?' he asked Ian and Tara.

'In there with the others,' Ian grinned. 'They won't be going anywhere in a hurry.'

'Great stuff. Go to the top of the class,' Zephyr laughed.

'Well, it was mostly Terra – she had the gang right where she wanted them,' Ian said.

'And the men back at the camp?' Tara asked.

'One is probably still drifting downstream scared out of his wits, the other is tied to a tree where we left him,' said Zephyr. 'We'd better get going – my uncle will be here any minute. The police can take it from here.'

'Any chance of me doing the driving?' Ian asked as he and Tara ran for the motorbike they'd left hiding under a bush.

'None whatsoever,' Tara replied.

Back at the camp, the four friends quickly changed back into their normal clothes, and buried their suits at the bottom of their bags. The motorbike was returned to the shed, its engine still warm. Then, doing their best to fight down the adrenalin that rushed through their bodies, they sat around the dining table, all of them talking at once.

They had done it. They had rescued Amir and Rajiv, stopped a tiger from being poached, and faced up to serious danger. And most important of all, they had survived unhurt. They couldn't wait to tell Mr Arturi everything. He'd probably have a heart attack.

'I'm going to need a holiday from this holiday,' April sighed. 'And we never did get to see a tiger.'

***

The tiger crept through the long grass, dark stripes breaking up the lines of its body. It kept low to the ground, panting gently. Stealing up on its prey. There, across the grassland was a herd of deer grazing quietly, ears twitching.

From the safety of the hide, Amir and the others held their breath, binoculars peeled. They'd been fortunate enough to spot this tiger on the last day of their trip – but to see one on the hunt, now that was something else.

The night before, Amir had come straight back to the campsite once he'd led the police to Hussein. When he saw Zaf and the others were safe, he'd broken down into tears of relief.

Amir had done his best to tell the four friends and the police everything he knew, about the poaching gang, his kidnapping, and his rescuers. But Amir had no way of explaining just how the poaching gang ended up in their own pit, surrounded by a ring of fire. It was all just too strange.

Hussein and his men were in jail awaiting trial – including one very wet and sorry-looking gang member who'd been pulled from the river miles downstream.

Zaf and the others had listened, suitable expressions of shock glued to their faces. 'Wow, Uncle,' said Zaf, 'it's hard to imagine – while all that was going on, we were just sitting around at the camp.'

A TIGER ON THE HUNT - THAT WAS **SOMETHING ELSE**.

'Wish we could have helped you in some way,' added April.

'I'm just so glad nothing happened to you,' said Amir.

Now, in the hide, Amir held his finger to his lips. They mustn't make a sound. Just watch.

The tiger inched forward, muscles rippling slowly under its proud coat. The deer lifted their heads suddenly, heads turning this way and that. They could sense something. They stopped chewing for a moment to listen. Then, satisfied that they were still alone on the plain, they went back to grazing.

With a spring from its powerful legs, the tiger lunged forward...

Chapter Fourteen

Home again

As predicted, back home at their hideout in the abandoned plane, Mr Arturi was in a state of total shock. He got up from his stool more than once to walk the floor. 'You're kidding me,' he said at last, taking off his glasses and wiping them where they'd got steamed up.

'I kid you not,' said Ian chuckling. 'I scorched that man's shoes something rotten.'

'I'm just so glad we got to see a tiger after all,' said Tara. 'And I feel a whole lot better knowing Hussein and his gang are out of business.'

Mr Arturi sighed. 'I wish we could say the same about all the tiger-smuggling rings out there. We can only hope they get stopped before it's too late.'

The plane fell silent for a moment.

Finally Zaf spoke up. 'Well, while there are people like my uncle out there, we have some hope, right?'

Mr Arturi smiled. 'True, true.' He patted Zaf on the back.

'So what's next for Factor Four?' Ian asked, rubbing his hands together. 'I'm getting a real taste for this superhero business. Blasting fireballs, catchy one-liners, rescuing my friends from total disaster.'

'Rescuing who?' Tara punched Ian on the shoulder.

Ian held up his hands in surrender. 'Just kidding,' he laughed.

'In all seriousness, I wanted to show you this,' said Mr Arturi. He pulled out a file from his desk and pushed it across the table to Zaf. 'This article came out while you were away.'

Zaf opened the file and pulled out a newspaper clipping. '"Cluna Sands Closed by Health Department",' he read aloud. '"Local beach and popular tourist destination Cluna Sands was this week closed by the authorities following the latest round of water quality testing, throwing the tourist season and seafood industry into jeopardy. Martin Johnson of the health board declined to give an explanation, saying that investigations into the matter were on-going."'

'But I swim there all the time!' April muttered.

'Well, I think we should do some investigating of our own,' said Mr Arturi. 'I don't want to be living in a place where the water is like poison.'

'No one should have to,' said Zaf. 'And if Factor Four have anything to say about it, no-one will.'

'Now, that sounds like a plan,' Ian grinned.

Find out how Factor 4 got their
superpowers and their mission in
Factor 4: The Awakening,
available now from A&C Black

First published 2013 by
A & C Black, an imprint of Bloomsbury Publishing Plc
50 Bedford Square, London, WC1B 3DP

www.acblack.com
www.bloomsbury.com

ISBN 978-1-4081-8185-0

A CIP catalogue for this book is available from the British Library.

Printed and bound by CPI Group (UK) Ltd, Croydon CR0 4YY

1 3 5 7 9 10 8 6 4 2

MIX
Paper from
responsible sources
FSC® C020471